Will It Be a Baby Brother?

Eve Bunting

Illustrated by **Beth Spiegel**

BOYDS MILLS PRESS

HONESDALE, PENNSYLVANIA

For Shane Davison Bunting
—*E.B.*

To my old friend Shirl: thanks for everything
—*B.S.*

My mom is having a baby.
I hope it's a boy, like me.

Mom has a book of names.
I helped her pick our favorites.
"*Sara*, if it's a girl," she says.
"*James*, if it's a boy."
"I like *James*," I mutter.

Grandma comes for dinner. "I want to start knitting," she says. "I'd like to get blue yarn for a boy or pink for a girl. But I guess I'll settle for yellow."

"Yellow's nice," Mom tells her.

I shake my head. "Blue's better."

Mom's friends give her a baby shower.
Everything she gets for the baby is white or yellow or green.
Even the little potty with the stars on it.
"What do *you* want, Edward?" Mom's friend asks me. "A boy or a girl?"

I shrug. "I want
a James."
Everyone laughs.

"You might only think you want a brother,"
Mom tells me. "But whichever it is, when you see it,
you'll know this was the kind you wanted all along."

"Uh-uh," I say.

I put the green potty with the stars
on it on my head. "I'm a spaceman,"
I shout. "James can be my space helper."

I rocket around the room till Mom
tells me to stop and be quiet.

That night, she spreads all my old baby clothes
on her bed beside the new things for the baby.
Dad and I come to see them.

Mom picks up a little red jacket and a cap shaped like a strawberry. "I remember you wearing this, Edward." She holds the jacket against me. "You were adorable."

"I don't like adorable." I squirm away before she can put the strawberry cap on my head. "James won't like adorable, either."

Dad grins. "What if James turns out to be Sara?"
I make a face. "I'll give her to Aunt Elizabeth."

Later I put my yellow dump truck and my wooden train into the crib that's waiting for James.

I put in my wheelbarrow that you can run with all around the house and fill with stuff, and my cowboy boots and my cowboy hat and my baseball mitt.

I move it all to the side so there'll be room for James, too.

"There," I tell him. "Everything's ready for you.
But hurry up and get here. I'm tired of waiting."

Not the next day,

or the next day,

but the day after that, our baby comes.
  "At last," I say.

Dad brings in the baby carrier,

and the baby looks up at me and smiles.
Honest.
I gasp. "Oh my gosh!"

And then, I can't help it.

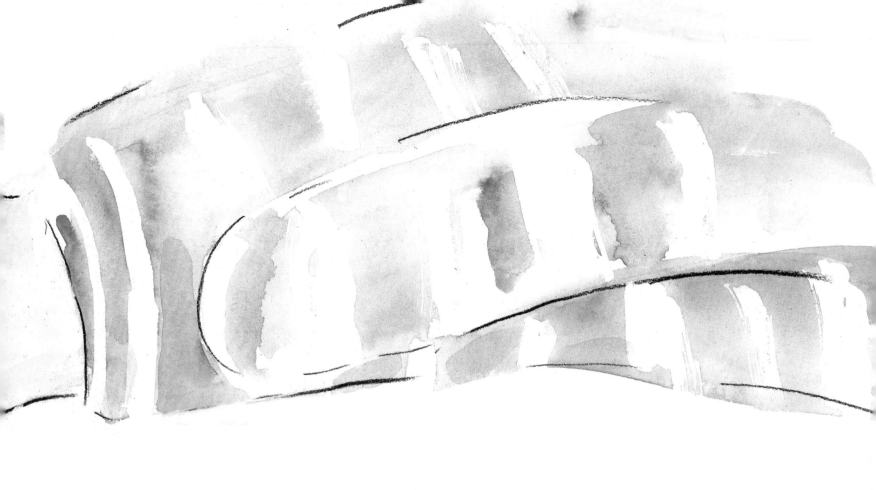

I bend down and kiss my little baby sister's
hand, and I feel all soppy and silly.

"She's pretty cool," I say.

And Mom was right. I *did* get
the kind I wanted all along—
even if I didn't know it.

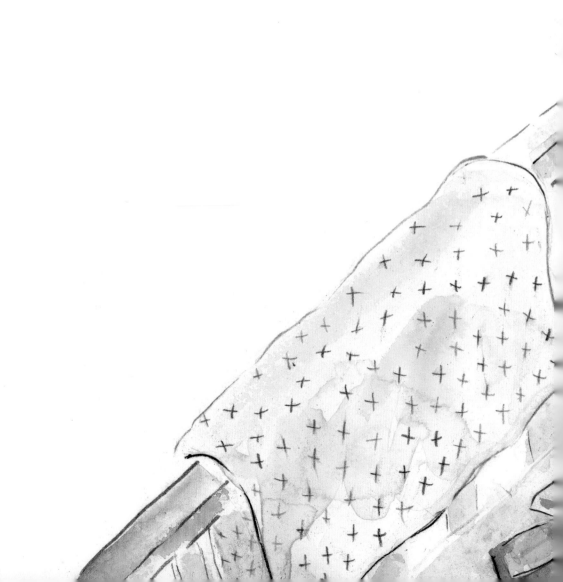

There's no way I'm going to give this baby to Aunt Elizabeth.
No way!

Text copyright © 2010 by Eve Bunting
Illustrations copyright © 2010 by Beth Spiegel

Boyds Mills Press, Inc.
815 Church Street
Honesdale, Pennsylvania 18431
Printed in the United States of America

Library of Congress Cataloging-in-Publication Data

Bunting, Eve
Will it be a baby brother? / Eve Bunting ; illustrated by Beth Spiegel. — 1st ed.
p. cm.
Summary: A little boy is certain that his expectant mother
will give birth to a baby brother.
ISBN 978-1-59078-439-6 (hardcover : alk. paper)
[1. Babies—Fiction. 2. Brothers and sisters—Fiction. 3. Family life—Fiction.]
I. Spiegel, Beth, ill. II. Title.
PZ7.B91527Wl 2010   [E]—dc22   2009025423

First edition
The text of this book is set in Goudy Old Style.
The illustrations are done in watercolor and pen and ink.

10 9 8 7 6 5 4 3
CPSIA facility code: BP 310075